WOODY AND JUNE VERSUS THE INFECTION

WOODY AND JUNE VERSUS THE INFECTION

WOODY AND JUNE VERSUS THE APOCALYPSE, EPISODE 11

ROBERT J. MCCARTER

LITTLE HUMMINGBIRD PUBLISHING

WOODY AND JUNE

VERSUS

THE APOCALYPSE

Woody and June versus the Infection

Woody and June versus the Apocalypse, Episode 11

Copyright © 2022 by Robert J. McCarter

Cover photography © 2020, Robert J. McCarter

"Zombies Ahead" image by ducu59us

Version 1.0, December 2022

ISBN: 978-1-941153-70-3

Find out more about this book at: WoodyAndJune.com

Visit Robert's website at: www.RobertJMcCarter.com

Published by:

Little Hummingbird Publishing

P.O. Box 23518

Flagstaff, AZ 86002

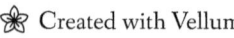 Created with Vellum

CHAPTER ONE

SURVIVAL IS NOT A PLAN, it's a goal. But we are learning that the apocalypse is a terrible place for plans. They don't survive the first encounter with zombies or the psychotic, petty, wannabe warlords. We make plans, June, Dallas, and I, but we have to be ready to abandon them at any moment for what seems like it will get us through the day... or the night.

And while the plans don't often survive, we want to.

The apocalypse is more like jazz—and forgive me here if I mangle this metaphor. While I enjoy jazz, I don't know that I understand it. But I do understand that it is about skill and preparation and improvisation. And that is exactly what survival is like now. You prepare, you plan as far ahead as you can see—which is generally not very far—and you improvise your butt off.

Take the three of us. June Medina is petite with short black hair, coffee-with-cream colored skin, and ocean-blue eyes. She's in her mid-twenties with a round face, an upturned nose, and looks rather like the kind of woman you would hire to play an elf around Christmas. Except she's a badass, ex-army, and deadly with a gun. And not bad at first aid either.

Then there is Dallas. She's older than us, in her early thirties and all curvy compared to June's lean athleticism. Dallas has a sharp wit, a ready laugh, and a foul mouth, with shoulder length brown hair and brown eyes. She was born and raised by a father, who would have been more comfortable with a son, in Montana, so she knows her ways around guns, loves the outdoors, and, despite her appearance, is something of a tomboy.

And then take me. My name is Woody Beckman and I'm a baseball-crazed Arizona boy. I'm the one with the weird plans and the one who knows how to rig electronics in this post-apocalyptic era.

To strain the jazz metaphor just a bit more, we are the Woody, June, and Dallas Post-Apocalyptic Survival Trio. And we have a hell of a survival challenge in front of us... or rather, behind us.

The zombie population of Winslow, Arizona is shambling towards us down Old Route 66. We aren't that far out of town, June and I taking turns pushing Dallas who is perched on an old-fashioned single-speed bike with a handlebar basket and a bell. She's got a swollen ankle she can't put any weight on. We are hoping it is just a sprain, but there is no way to tell yet.

We survived Winslow, and the trap Talia—June's ex and the psychotic, petty, wannabe warlord who just can't let us go—set for us, but we are not free. We are in the middle of Talia's "game," one that seems to be designed to kill Dallas and me—in the most horrible way possible—somehow forcing June to go back to Talia.

As if.

But then again Talia has earned both the "psychotic" and "petty" in her title, so perhaps expecting logic is not realistic.

June and I entered Winslow to rescue Dallas in a well-supplied Toyota pickup truck and we left with Dallas unable to walk, with only our guns, a rifle, a bat, our backpacks, and a bike.

But we improvised and we survived.

The problem is that Talia is improvising too. And she has resources and manpower and the luxury of not being on the run all the time, not being injured.

Winslow is high desert, just below five-thousand-feet in elevation and fairly flat, the parched land mostly covered with dried grass, a bit of it still green from spring, and scraggly bushes. To our right are some train tracks and then, basically, nothing for a long ways. To our left, just out of sight, is I-40 and just off the highway we can see a Denny's that, as I recall, is attached to a truck stop. My stomach rumbles and a grand slam breakfast sounds like heaven this far into the apocalypse.

Behind us is the Winslow zombie horde, thousands strong, their collective fungus mind telling them that we are the only fresh meat in town.

They can sense us, it is what has made them so effective, and when they run out of prey, they gather and their senses are that much better.

Up ahead is a low warehouse-looking building that I stare at for a moment as I push Dallas along. I know what it is but my brain is sluggish. We don't have time to fish out a pair of binoculars from one of our packs, so I start pushing harder.

"Woody...?" June asks. "What is it?"

"There are a lot of cars there," I say, and then it hits me. This is a car dealership. "A lot of cars," I say grinning.

Transportation is what we need the most. We need to get away from Talia. We need to get away from the horde of zombies. Dallas can't walk. There is nothing we need more.

And I will admit that I am still shell-shocked from Winslow. Literally shell-shocked having been in the close proximity of multiple explosions.

I push harder. "I'll go try to find us a vehicle," I say to June, "while you keep moving with Dallas."

She's jogging easily beside me. I'm in better aerobic shape than when the world went to shit, but I'm not in the kind of shape June is in. She doesn't seem to be that bothered by the smoke inhalation from this morning in the Apache Death Caves.

Just this morning. It's so hard to fathom so much has happened. The sun is high above us and the day isn't even half over yet.

I can see from the twist of her lips that she doesn't like the plan, that she doesn't want us to be separated, that she's still going through something with what happened back in Winslow.

This is still day twenty-seven of Woody and June versus the Apocalypse. When we met at the pet food plant in Flagstaff, Arizona, we were both go-it-alone survivors. But then she saved my life and I returned the favor and rescued her from the Flagstaff psychotic, petty, wannabe warlord and we learned to trust each other. And then we became partners in survival, and then after all that went down in the Grand Canyon after Talia captured us, we fell in love.

Well, I fell for her that first day, but I think it took her a bit longer. Back in Winslow I had been surrounded, no chance of escape, when she plowed our truck into the horde, risking her own life and giving me a fighting chance and dragging me out of there.

That was an hour ago and what we need is time to rest and recover and talk it through. In these twenty-seven short days, I've lost her twice, I've fought like hell to get her back, and I know some of what she must be going through.

But then her mouth twists into a strange little smile and she nods. "Be safe, Woody," she says, her voice quiet. She takes over pushing Dallas, and I pull my bat from the holster I rigged on my backpack and jog off across the median towards the dealership.

"And get something nicer than a damn truck," Dallas calls. "I want to ride in style."

CHAPTER TWO

WHEN I WAS on my own, after I escaped the mess in Phoenix, I wouldn't have approached a place like this by myself. And if I did, if I was desperate enough, I would be very slow and methodical.

So, the Zs congregate as they run out of food, but that doesn't mean there aren't Zs trapped in the dealership. In fact, I have to assume there are. And I have to go into the dealership to get keys and hope that one of these vehicles will actually start. It's been over a year since it all went to shit, so the odds there aren't great.

And the snarling, stinking zombie horde shambling towards me severely limits the amount of time I have here, making this even longer odds, but I have to try.

I hate to break up our improvising survival trio. I don't want to do the solo stuff anymore. I want to be with my people. We all have different strengths, we are stronger together.

All of these thoughts run through my mind as I jog over, bat in hand, puffs of dirt floating up as I trot across the open field on my way to the dealership.

It's one of those multi-brand dealerships you see in small towns. One sign says "Chrysler. Jeep. Dodge," the other one "Nissan."

As I get closer, the building looks a little less like a warehouse.

There are some brick columns out front supporting the white metal roof, a glass along the front, and a single tree making it clear that it's not a warehouse. Not flashy, but then again, they don't need to impress me with fancy digs, free coffee, and Wi-Fi. A zombie-free environment and a battery that still has a charge will impress me more than anything.

As I approach, I realize how foolish this is, this little improvisation I proposed. Back in Flagstaff, when I got the truck that was just blown up, I got lucky. The truck I wanted wouldn't start but I found a fresh battery that had just enough charge to jump it with. And this is my area. This is the kind of thing I should think about before going off alone.

As I approach the car lot, I look over and can see that June is pushing Dallas and watching me. I give her a cheerful wave and slow down as I hit the pavement of the lot.

Except for the dust and dirt all over everything, you might think that things are normal, that it is just a Sunday and a dust storm blew through town and no one has been around to clean it up.

Trucks, for the most part, line the front of the lot. Full-size Dodges and then the smaller Nissans. Each way more than I could afford in the pre-apocalyptic times.

I walk past them to the front of the warehouse-like building and look in the glass.

Inside it's open with a truck and a sedan on display along with cubicles for the salespeople. It looks empty, no signs of Zs. I knock on the glass. I want them to know I am here. But nothing happens.

I move to the door and open it slowly. A puff of chilly air floats out that smells just a little bit like a new car, that plasticky smell. I stop and listen. Nothing. Zs are not known for being quiet.

The cement-floored showroom has the two cars and there are three cubicles for doing the paperwork. At the back of the building is a hallway, probably back to service, and a row of glass-walled offices.

It's quiet in here and cool. There's a layer of dust on everything, but otherwise it looks fairly normal. The cubicle closest to me has some paperwork neatly laid out as if they'll all be right back to complete the purchase.

This is the apocalypse—there are plenty of pockets of almost normal that can just absolutely creep you out. I'd frankly be more at ease if the place was trashed, if some survivors had come through scrounging and left it a mess. It's too close to normal. This orderly and neat stuff isn't the world anymore.

I shake it off and head to the back row of offices, to the first one. The keys to all these lovely cars are probably in one of them. I need to grab a bunch and see if any of these cars are alive.

The horde is coming, and I don't want to be in this building when they get here. I'm moving too fast, but I have to. I pull open the glass door and step halfway in before I see her.

Talia.

She's sitting behind the broad wooden desk in the plush office chair, a smirk on her lean face. "So... you're interested in a new car, eh, Mr. Beckman," she says with her mild southern drawl and nods. "Have a seat. Let's talk terms."

CHAPTER THREE

I DON'T KNOW her last name. She's one of those one name only figures and doesn't need two names. Talia. June's ex and our nemesis.

She looks rested and relaxed and fed. She's wearing a blue down jacket, one of those thin ones, that fits her wiry frame well. She's taller than me with hazel eyes and sandy blond hair that is shaved on the sides and pulled back into a tight ponytail. Her left eye has an ugly purple bruise from the fight she and June got in. That part makes me feel a little better.

I want to kill her. Right now. With my bat. I've never killed the living before and I never thought I would want to. But she is worse than a zombie. She is sick. She is psychotic. And she loves the apocalypse.

"Oh, no you don't," she says, slowly pulling her hands up so that I can see them. She's got a gun in her right hand and a taser in her left. "Sit. Down. Now." She gestures with the gun.

I step forward, letting the door shut behind me with a swish against the short grey carpet. It's cold in here and I don't have a jacket, a chill passing through me.

I pull the chair back and sit, my grip on my bat tightening, my knuckles going white. I'm perched on the edge of my seat (yes, quite literally) because of the backpack I have on.

"I was hoping it would be my June-bug that came," she says as she leans back, gesturing out towards the road casually with the taser. "That she would come to her senses and we could end all this. But I knew one of you two would be over."

She sighs dramatically but I don't answer. The scratches on my hands and forearms that I got when June dragged me out of the Winslow zombie horde are itching like crazy and I want to get the hell out of here, but that wouldn't be playing Talia's game. She punishes you if you don't play her game. Like when she captured Dallas and chained her to the statue of Glenn Frey on the corner in Winslow.

"Not talkative, I see," she says. "I took your vehicle away and here you are trying to replace it. Not good." She tsks at me like I'm some four-year-old that just ate his own booger. "Here's the deal, though, since I am a reasonable woman. I'll trade you a working vehicle for one broken bone. My choice."

My jaw drops open. "What...? You want to...?"

"I want to break one of your bones, Woody," she says with a cheerful smile. "I think I'd feel a lot better if I did, and you would have a vehicle."

It's not lost on me that she is saying "vehicle" not "car" or "truck." And "working vehicle" could be a clunker with little life left in it and less gas.

"Which bone?" I ask. I don't understand the way she thinks.

She shrugs and smiles. "I haven't decided yet, but you'll be able to drive after I'm done with you."

This is definitely part of her sick, little game. Trying to force us into choices, difficult choices, horrible choices. The choice in Winslow was for June and me to leave Dallas to the zombies or die. But we managed a third choice, and I think she's pissed about it. There was not supposed to be three of us anymore.

A broken bone—which Dallas could have right now—is quite

nearly a death sentence in this environment. I could drive with a broken leg if it was an automatic, or a broken rib, or even a broken arm. My mind's slipping, trying to understand what she is offering here, what she is doing. And there is no way she'd let me off with only a broken rib.

"And if I refuse?" I ask.

She shrugs again. "Then you are not playing the game anymore and you must suffer the consequences of trying to replace your vehicle."

Dallas refused to enter the Apache Death Cave in Two Guns. She wasn't playing the game anymore. She was captured and chained to a statue right before Talia unleashed the Winslow zombie horde.

"You never said anything about not using a vehicle," I say as I slowly ease my gun out of its holster, rolling my shoulders and stretching my neck to hide the motion.

She leans forward, her eyes connecting with mine. "I shouldn't have to. My game. My rules. I win."

"I think I need to think it over," I say, attempting a smile while I keep the gun under the desk and point it at her. "Can I get back to you on this?"

"Sure," she says happily. "But no decision is a decision. You have five seconds. Broken bone and a vehicle or you are not playing the game anymore."

She counts down slowly as I press the gun to the cheap particle board on the back of the desk. I've got it pointed at her abdomen and there is no way I can miss.

"Five... Four... Three... Two..."

On "one," I fire.

CHAPTER FOUR

THIS IS TALIA'S GAME. It's rigged. She's been ahead of us every step of the way. Including this one.

The sound of my gun firing under the desk is loud in the small room, setting my damaged ears to rigging again. The gun kicks back a little, the desk shutters, and I can smell smoke, but nothing happens. Talia just sits there and smiles.

"I didn't think you had it in you, Woody," she says, nodding like some kind of approving parent. "I really didn't."

"What...?" I mumble, confused. There is no way I could have missed. There was only cheap particle board between us. Our guns have been on us the whole time, Talia couldn't have tampered with them.

She leans back and kicks the back of the desk and I hear the muffled ring of metal. "I ain't stupid, you know," she says. "And I guess you've made your choice. It's a goddamn miracle that bullet didn't ricochet and kill you."

They prepared. They reinforced the desk. They expected this.

She straightens her arm, the one holding the taser, and fires, the little darts penetrating my shirt and electricity coursing through my body as I spasm on the chair. It hurts. God, it hurts. I don't have control over my muscles. I'm flopping around like a fish. I am as good as dead. Talia can break any bone she wants, or all my bones.

I am vaguely aware of Talia moving, and then I hear her say, "Goodnight, Mr. Woodpecker. Don't worry, the game is not over yet, the girls are getting their next clue right about now. You know... you don't look so good. Those scratches you got escaping, just ain't right, are they?" She sighs. "Not my problem, Woodpecker. Just play the game and there still might be a chance for you. I mean, I doubt it, but you never know." And then she hits me in the head with the butt of her gun and it all goes dark.

DAYS like this you don't survive. You just don't.

First smoke inhalation and a very strange zombie fight in the Apache Death Caves. And then fighting thousands of Zs with dynamite and a baseball bat in Winslow. Followed by an explosion at the Winslow 9-11 memorial. And now being tasered and pistol-whipped.

You just don't survive.

But I do wake up. Slowly. Painfully. Regretfully. I wake up.

My head hurts like hell and the sun is bright... too bright. My wrists hurt and my hands are tingling numb, my arms pulled back behind me. I'm sitting down on something cool and there is something behind me supporting my back and also digging into it. I smell blood and my mouth tastes sour, like terrible morning breath.

I try to open my eyes, but it's too bright, so I take a deep breath and listen. I scan my body looking for broken bones.

My forehead is throbbing with each heartbeat near my left temple, each breath, each movement a sharp pain in my head. My left arm still hurts from the bullet wound. My forehead itches from another bullet wound. The recent zombie scratches on my forearms and hands burn. I'm dizzy and nauseous. I'm tired. I'm hungry. I'm dehydrated. Those last three are just par for the course these days.

I slit my eyes open and see the desert. Pale, sandy soil like there used to be limestone here, scattered weeds, some still green from spring rain. Some of these weeds are pretty big, looking like they will become tumbleweed. There's a gentle breeze and it's warmer than it was in Winslow.

Talia didn't kill me. But then again, she could have killed all of us many times. I know she wants me dead, but she wants it done in a particular way. In her way.

I press back and the surface behind me gives a little and I hear a metallic ring and feel metal digging into my back. It's a fence. My hands are cuffed behind me.

I lean forward, try to pull my hands away, but I can't. It seems the handcuffs are attached to the fence. I feel with my fingers and touch the cool metal of the fence and find the padlock attaching the hand-cuffs to the fence.

I pull again, harder, but the pain in my head multiplies, the world spins, and I puke out what little I have left in my stomach, leaving my throat raw, the sour scent of it overwhelming the iron scent of blood.

My head down, I slit my eyes open a little more and I see... desert. Just desert, the land sloping gently down in front of me. I slowly raise my eyes, careful not to move too fast, and I see two cuts in the land. There's pavement—it must be I-40. Beyond the highway I see a line of denser and greener vegetation. There must be water there, a drainage of some sort. To my right, just in front of the highway, I see a small ramshackle building, the shingles gone and the wood of the roof decaying.

I take slow breaths and gently turn my head to get a wider view. A few more buildings off in the distance, too far away to see much detail. I twist around and catch a glimpse of the fence, a small rectangular building, a shed really, and a metal tower.

It's a cell tower. It has to be. Talia dragged me out here and cuffed me to this fence. No food. No water. No hope.

There's a barely-there dirt road leading to the tower and down to the highway and nothing else. No noise but the breeze. No motion that I can see. And then I spot my backpack sitting on the ground five yards away.

What the hell? I had it on when she knocked me out, but they left it with me? Why would she do that?

I struggle, trying to lever myself up, my arms stretching behind me, the metal fence ringing, but it's no good. I'm dizzy and nearly puke again. Besides, that's a padlock attaching the cuffs to the fence, there is nothing I can do. I collapse back to the ground. I am as vulnerable as Dallas was this morning. A single Z wandering through could take me out. A hungry coyote could take me out. Time will take me out.

I feel bad about how we teased Dallas when she was still chained to the statue after we had dragged her and the statue away from that famous corner in Winslow.

And then I'm thinking about Dallas with her injured ankle and June pushing her along on the bike with thousands of Zs shambling after them.

I left them to go get a car. I didn't come back.

I remember what Talia said after she tasered me, "The girls are getting their next clue right about now."

This is part of the game.

I'm part of the game.

June has been rescued twice. We just rescued Dallas. It looks like it's my turn to be rescued. I just hope they can figure the clue out. It's not like I'm on the site of a famous song like Dallas was. I don't know where the hell I am.

I look around more. High desert. Fairly flat. Weeds and a bit of grass. I could be almost anywhere between Two Guns and Holbrook. But no. I look up at the sun. It's afternoon now, but not that far into afternoon. And the only waterway close to I-40 around here is the Little Colorado River, which is close to the highway between Winslow and Holbrook. Since June and Dallas only have a bike for transportation, if they are going to find me, I sure as hell better be close to Winslow.

That is my hope and I cling to it as I sit there beneath a dead cell tower waiting for rescue.

CHAPTER FIVE

BEING the rescuee instead of the rescuer is kind of boring. Nerve-racking, but boring. And I have time to think and feel miserable—way too much time for both.

I should have drawn on Talia as soon as I saw her, but that would have been stupid. I hate guns. Because of what happened with my brother when we were kids, I have always avoided them, even post-apocalypse. June just taught me how to use one and Talia is well-trained ex-army. I wouldn't have stood a chance.

We shouldn't have stopped. Not at the rim of the Grand Canyon. Not at Wupatki. Not for those two lovely days in the Earthship in the 40s. Not at Meteor Crater. We should have run far and fast and not stopped until we got to the White Mountains.

But that's stupid. Get tired and you make mistakes. Stupid mistakes. How were we supposed to know that Talia would follow us out of the canyon so quickly and get control over the East Flagstaff survivors and come after us like this.

Survival doesn't often leave time for reflection, but I had too much time now. My butt against the cool ground, my back against the chain-link fence, the sun slowly arching across the sky as I get thirsty and hungry, as my head throbs and my stomach roils and my hands go completely numb from the tight handcuffs. It doesn't take me long to realize that I have a concussion. That I am in bad shape. That I don't even know if I can walk.

My mind winds over and over what has happened since we met Talia and how I somehow should have done a better job. I should have gotten us away from Talia. I should have taken care of June and Dallas.

Yeah, I know, kind of misogynistic and ignoring the fact that they were involved in all the decisions and both of them are better equipped for the apocalypse than I am. It also ignores the fact that at Meteor Crater the three of us decided together that we would try to go back to the Grand Canyon knowing just how long the odds were.

But that's what the mind does in a situation like this. I'm afraid and my mind is reflecting that, busy judging my actions. Harshly.

We took those breaks because we were beat to hell and exhausted. Because safety is rare in the apocalypse. Because if you are tired you will make stupid mistakes and we had no way of knowing what was coming.

Our decision to go back to the Grand Canyon was an act of compassion. Those people wouldn't stand a chance once Talia turned her attention back on them.

But that logic is a small voice among the torrent of judgements.

I then start wondering if it is really possible to escape handcuffs if you break your thumb, like in the movies. This is, admittedly, a desperate distraction from self-recrimination, and I need it, so I go there.

But how the hell would I break my thumb, and what the hell would I actually be breaking, and does this have something to do with Talia offering to give me a vehicle if I let her break one of my bones? Was that a clue she gave me or was she just planting a seed in hopes that I do something really stupid?

Back in Winslow when Dallas was chained to the statue and the horde was coming, Dallas begged me to end her life before the Zs got her. I offered to chop her hand off because it was the only thing I could think of, but she refused. She would rather be dead than maimed. Which makes sense. You get injured that badly and you probably are dead. And she was terrified of becoming a Z and saw no way out, thus her wanting me to kill her.

As I sat there and contemplated all of this, that is the thought that possessed me. I die out here cuffed to the fence, I become a Z. Whether it's from dehydration or a coyote or a Z munching on me, I die, I become a Z.

I faced this when I was alone. The fungal infection is in all of us —you die, you are a Z. Unless you blow your own head off. I look down slowly and my gun is still there.

It takes a moment for my concussed brain to register it.

I have a gun.

I also have my hands cuffed behind me.

I twist around, sliding my butt on the dirt, slouching down so my belt is at the level of my hands, and get the right side of my waist near my hands. My heart starts beating rapidly and the world starts spinning, but I keep going, my fingers finding the cool metal. Never in my life was I so glad to come in contact with a gun.

My spine is twisted uncomfortably, but I get a little bit of a grip and pull and my hand slips off.

I grunt, twisting myself more, the fence dully ringing from pressing against it, and try again... and fail again.

I close my eyes so I can't see the world spin and swallow hard against my rising gorge and reach again. Slowly, carefully and... the gun comes free and I am exhausted.

I untwist myself and switch the gun into my right hand. I'm panting like I just sprinted around all three bases for a home run and a smile cracks my face.

It's not much. The gun is held awkwardly behind me and I'll have to twist again to shoot it, and I don't even know if Talia left it loaded. But it's something. It gives options. Really stupid options, but I have a chance of defending myself.

I smile despite the pain in my head. It feels like someone is driving a nail into it, and then reality fades as I slip into a troubled sleep.

CHAPTER SIX

I WAKE UP WITH A START, my pulse pounding, the pain in my head spiking, and I don't know where I am. Did I hear voices? Is that what woke me up?

The press of the fence against my back, the smell of vomit and dried blood, the abandoned highway and the darker green swath snaking past beyond it bring me back.

Talia cuffed me to the fence around a cell tower somewhere between Winslow and Holbrook. The sun has moved, but not all that much. I slept about an hour.

My hands are numb, my face flushed hot, and I worry that the sun is burning my freckled face now that I don't have a hat.

I hear it again, a voice. A rough female voice. Too far away for me to make out the words, but my heart leaps. I know that voice. June.

"Here!" I shout, or try to shout, my mouth so dry and my tongue thick and my voice just a croak. "Here!" I try again, getting more volume. "June, I'm here!"

I feel moisture on my face and realize that I am crying, that is how relieved I am. June and Dallas found me. Somehow they found me.

I keep shouting, "Here! I'm here!" my voice slowly getting

stronger until I hear a change in the calling voice, a hopeful tone, but I still can't make her words out.

I shout and then listen and I shout again. She is getting closer. I am nauseous and dizzy, and it's bad, but not quite as bad as before I slept.

I see movement on the highway coming closer. I'm low to the ground so it's just a glimpse, and I start yelling louder, my voice rough, my dry throat hurting.

And then I see movement closer, coming from my left, from the opposite direction of June.

Shit.

Again it's just a glimpse, but it's the characteristic shambling motion of a Z.

Shit!

It's one, maybe two, and I must have been out of its fresh-brains radar range, but all the shouting has roused it. What am I going to do? There's a few minutes and I must not panic.

I take a deep breath and close my eyes against the rising dizziness. Do the math in my head. June is quicker, but the zombies are closer and she doesn't know exactly where I am. Maybe I'm still out of range of the Zs, but no, they've locked on.

I remember the gun, my fingers feeling for it on the ground, but shooting it like this is dangerous. I open my eyes, turn my head, and look for the Zs and don't see them. Was I imagining it?

June's call comes again, high-pitched and desperate. And there's another voice I can make out, Dallas. Brief relief washes over me knowing that they are okay. But I don't yell back, not yet. I need to think.

I slowly turn my head so I can look at the fence. It's made out of thick metal wire, woven together in a diamond pattern, the bottom tip has the wire curved back and locking with the other wire. Each diamond is two wires bent and woven top to bottom. It's simple. It's strong. And with me being padlocked to it, I can't just pull myself free. Unless...

I study the portion I can see and feel with my hands. They padlocked my hands low, just one diamond up, and that means if I could unlock the bottom wires, pull it free, untwist it enough, I should be able to free myself. But how?

The calls come again and I see another flash of shuffling movement, this time closer. Yes, the Zs are locked on to me, so noise doesn't matter.

"June! Dallas!" I shout. "I'm here. Quick!" But my voice is still weak, my tongue thick.

I get my mostly numb fingers around that bent back portion of wire below where I'm cuffed and pull. It does no good. Calling this metal "wire" is misleading. I mean, it is a cylindrical extrusion of metal, but it's not pliable copper but hard steel. It is bendable, but I don't have leverage with my fingers.

I keep shouting every ten seconds or so, but my focus has shifted. To go back to the jazz ensemble metaphor, while my band members are getting ready to join me, this is my solo. It's time for me to improvise around the theme of our piece. They may get here in time, but that is not the way to conduct yourself in this world anymore. I have to act like they won't get here in time.

I push back the dizziness and my rising nausea. I breathe slow and steady. I think. I have the gun and can try to shoot while sitting here and my hands are cuffed behind my back, but if I could just get free, I could run or I could get my hands in front of me and really shoot.

But I need leverage to bend the wire. The gun is metal, strong, but too clumsy. I've got a long thin knife on my left hip, but that would just be stupid. And then it hits me, and I realize how sluggish my brain has been since Talia knocked me out. "Leatherman," I whisper to myself.

BATMAN WOULD APPROVE of us survivors. You wear a belt and you hang things on your belt. Gun. Knife. Flashlight. Leatherman. You can't be fumbling in your pockets and you can't think about having such essentials with you.

I scoot down and to the other side, getting my cuffed hands to my left side, flip up the Velcro on the little sheath that holds the Leatherman, my fingers finding the cool metal of the multi-tool. If my hands weren't so numb, this would be a whole lot easier. Why did Talia cuff me so tightly but leave me armed? Did she actually think this through? Is this part of her "game," giving me a chance to free myself?

When she took Dallas and chained her to the statue in Winslow, she gave us a time limit. After that the Winslow zombie horde was released.

Shit. I should have thought of this sooner. I may have just killed myself with that nap. What is wrong with me?

I shout again, this time, I can hear the panic in my voice, and I swear I can hear the scrape of a foot against the ground. But I don't turn. I focus. I pull the Leatherman out, I open it up so it's a set of pliers, I drop it...

As my hands fish for the tool, I slowly turn so I don't get too dizzy and see them. Three Zs. They are getting close now, about fifty yards away, maybe two minutes.

"June! Dallas!" I shout. "Incoming. Now would be good!"

I close my eyes, the pliers in one hand and my fingers feeling with the other. If they weren't so numb this wouldn't be too bad. I guide the pliers in, clamp down, and twist.

Chain-link fences are strong. It's the weaving of the metal strands that make it so strong. But even one of those strands is pretty darn strong. I twist, but nothing. I shift my grip, so I have both hands on it, and twist again and... it moves, a little.

I feel again with one hand, the end of the wire moved about ten degrees. I slip the pliers farther in now that there is room and shift back to the two-handed grip.

My eyes are closed to help me visualize what I can't see. I let out a breath and listen... I can definitely hear the Zs shambling now, their feet scraping across the desert as they close in on me. There's not much time.

I hear the shouts of June and Dallas, but they are not close enough. I know I should still be calling for them, but that would delay me here. And I have to get free of this fence. I have to.

I squeeze and twist with all I've got, grunting from the effort, ignoring the increasing dizziness and nausea, and the wire moves.

I open my eyes. The Zs are twenty yards away. I feel the metal and the one is open about forty degrees, but I'm not sure if that's enough. My body tells me it's time for flight, that I should pull for all that I'm worth, that it's my only chance for survival, but I ignore it.

Yes, the bottom of the diamond could separate now, but I have to get past the twist of the two wires at the top of the diamond and the pliers won't help with that.

I close my eyes again, move the pliers to the other wire, grip, and do the two-handed twist. My hands are weak and I almost lose my grip. I take a moment to listen again, the Zs are closer, but not on me. I tighten my grip, take a deep breath, and twist and... I feel the metal moving.

I drop the Leatherman. There's no more time. I feel and both pieces of metal are bent enough that the bottom of the diamond has no strength anymore. I find the gun, grip it in my numb fingers, open my eyes, and lean forward.

The Zs are ten yards away, their snarling, shuffling, snapping jaw sounds loud in my ears, their rotting meat, fungal scent filling my nose. The sun is beating down on me, my face hot and my head spiking in pain with every rapid heartbeat.

I let my body's fight or flight instinct take over. I grunt and shout as I lean forward, my arms being pulled painfully behind me, the cuffs cutting into my wrists, my heart beating so loudly and painfully in my head that I can barely hear the Zs.

My problem is leverage. I'm sitting on the ground, my legs crossed. I don't have the force needed to untwist the top of the diamond.

Five yards.

I scramble, getting into a kneeling position, wedging my feet underneath me, the gun still in my hand. My brain, my stupid brain, reminds me of Talia's "you use guns, we use guns" rule. But that doesn't matter. Only survival matters now.

I press my back against the fence and then shove myself hard forward, the fence dully ringing, my head spinning and the pain spiking, my nausea rising, my arms stretching behind me painfully.

Nothing.

I do it again, shoving harder. And again. And again.

The Zs are almost on me and I have a choice. Shoot with my hands behind my back, having little chance of hitting them, or give it one last try.

I'm not a great shot in the best of circumstances, so I take a deep breath and give it everything I've got. I throw myself away from the fence, rocking forward enough so I can shove with my feet. A guttural cry escapes me and the tough steel wire finally gives way, and I go tumbling just as the lead zombie gets to where I was.

It's not much. I bought myself a few seconds, my hands still cuffed behind my back, but at least I am free of the fence. Except the world is spinning and I need to throw up, the smell of the Zs only making that worse, and I'm on the ground not really knowing which way is up.

This is it. This is the end. And I don't have any startling moments of clarity. I don't suddenly see my life and its many challenges as some sort of pristine creation that makes sense in retrospect.

I'm injured and hurt and desperate for survival. The lead Z, an older man with short grey hair and half his cheek dangling from his face, reaches me before I've even got my bearings. He's reaching down and I don't think. I kick, my boot catching him in the chest and he stumbles back. He's fairly desiccated, not well fed, but at this point, he's probably a lot stronger than me. He stumbles back into the other two Zs and I scramble up, the world spinning around me.

By some miracle, I've still got the gun, but using it seems silly. I am vaguely aware of a voice calling, getting louder, but I don't have any attention to spare.

I need to get my hands in front of me. I stumble away, my steps as hesitant and as shambling as a Z. The world is spinning around me. I am not right.

I hear the snarling, snapping jaws close to me, my steps taking me away from the fence towards the highway across the open desert.

I focus on the ground, try to will the world from spinning so much, keep my feet moving one step and then two and then three. This is my plan, this is my solo, to stumble away from the Zs, to keep alive for another moment or two, another breath or two.

I need to keep a hold of the gun. I need to get my hands in front of me. I need to find June.

June.

The thought is a spark, a light in my beleaguered brain. I need to get to June. I can hear her shouting, it's getting closer. I look up, trying to find her, but that makes the dizziness worse, so I keep focused on the ground, keep my feet moving, keep a hold of the gun, but change my path to head towards her voice.

I don't speak. I can't. This is all I can do. Stumble toward her voice and keep my feet moving, keep ahead of the three Zs behind me.

I don't know how long this goes on. I am not well enough or sane enough. The pain in my head is nearly unbearable, spiking with each heartbeat. I am sweating and so hot, my numb hands barely able to keep a grip on the gun.

But I do realize I don't hear her anymore and that the sound of the Zs has faded just a little. I slow my stumbling walk and look up and I see her. Her ocean-blue eyes are wide and her mouth is open as if she were trying to find the right words. She's got a gun in each hand and they are raised, ready to fire, and they are pointed right at me.

My brain struggles and I open my mouth to speak, but my tongue is so thick and my mouth so dry that just a groan comes out.

She takes a step back, a strangled "no" escaping her beautiful lips as she shakes her head, her short black hair plastered to her head with sweat, her breath coming fast from a long run.

And then I finally have my moment of clarity. I've been shambling towards her, stumbling, not speaking. She thinks I'm a Z.

She raises her guns and I know in my gut she's going to fire.

CHAPTER SEVEN

IN TALIA'S SCHEMING PSYCHOTIC, petty, wannabe warlord mind, this is what she wants. For June to gun me down thinking I am a Z. For me to bleed and die like one of the living and for her to realize it. For this tragedy to be her revenge.

She couldn't have planned it to happen this way, here, today. There are just too many variables. But in her twisted little heart I just know this is what she wants. This is her best outcome. This is the goal of this stupid "game" she's been playing with us.

I stop, standing there blinking, trying to get my mouth to work, but it is so dry and my tongue is so thick that I know it will be no more than a grunt, that it will further confirm what June fears. That I am a zombie.

I hear the Zs getting closer, smell their fetid bouquet. There is no time. I can see in June's blue eyes that she doesn't want to shoot me but believes that she must. She is only delaying on the thin hope that she is wrong, giving me scant seconds to prove that I am not a fresh Z.

Besides speaking, what can I do to prove that to her? Instantly. The thought doesn't so much occur to me as my dizziness and nausea become insurmountable. I give in to them, not that I have much choice.

As June's face hardens, as she expels her breath getting ready to squeeze the trigger of her two guns, I let go. I fall. I puke. I demonstrate my living status in the most messy of ways, but the only way I can anymore.

I hear the loud bark of her two guns as I hit the ground as I give in to the pain and the nausea and the dizziness, as I fall to my knees and puke, not that there is much of anything left in my stomach to come up.

There is a third shot and then silence, no more snarling Zs, although I can still smell them and that just makes my guts heave more.

Sometime later, I am sitting on the ground panting, my hand free from the cuffs and sipping from a water bottle June has given me. Dallas is visible on the dirt road to the cell tower slowly hobbling with the bike.

"You look like shit, Woody," June says. "I almost blew your head off."

I nod and try to smile. The water is helping a little. I can finally talk. "I... I feel like shit," I croak.

Something is wrong with me. Something beyond being hit on the head. My hands and arms are swollen, the long scratches from the zombies angry and red and weeping, there are large indents in my wrists where the cuffs were. Talia didn't make the cuffs too tight, my arms swelled after they left me.

All those scratches I got escaping the Zs in Winslow, when June plowed the truck into me and dragged me out, they are making me sick.

My head still hurts badly. I'm still dizzy and nauseous. This is not good.

"I... I think maybe I'm infected," I say.

June purses her lips so tightly they almost disappear and slowly nods. This is not something I've seen before. Anyone that got in the kind of trouble I was in never recovered.

"What do we do?" she asks.

I shake my head. "The horde?" I ask.

She sighs. "Talia's clue was for shit. 'Go east to where the rabbit runs and your boyfriend will be in the tallest tree.'" She shakes her head. "And she gave us three hours. The first part was fine. It took us, like, fifteen damn miles on that bike to find the Jack Rabbit Trading Post back there." Her thumb stabs back towards Dallas who is slowly maneuvering herself and the bike over the desert towards us.

"I cut out the front of the basket," she continues, "and Dallas rode while I pedaled. But the 'tallest tree' crap fooled us. We went back and forth for over an hour screaming our lungs out looking for you, looking up every damn tree along the canyon. No idea it was a cell tower until we heard you."

"Sorry," I say. "I passed out. I'm guessing that small group of Zs was on a timed release."

She shrugs as if to say it doesn't matter, because it doesn't.

"What now?" I ask. I'm too sick to come up with a plan, especially not one that involves Dallas who can't walk and me when I don't even know if I can stand.

She smiles and puts the back of her hand to my forehead. She sighs. "You are burning up. Can you stand? Can you walk?"

I try to smile and shrug. She helps me up, but the world spins and I just cling to her. "I think that's a no," I say.

"Okay," she says. "No working vehicles back at the trading post, and Dallas's ankle is still swelling and it's getting dangerous with that cuff on it, so it's time for plan B."

"Plan B?" I ask.

She nods up at the cell tower and the fenced-in area which is six feet tall with razor wire on top. As my gaze wanders up the tower, I see something, something that shouldn't be there. It looks like a goddamn treehouse about fifty feet up built into the metal latticework of the tower. A rough wooden platform made out of a hodge-podge of wood, some of it bare, most of it painted different colors.

The tower is three-sided, wide at the base, about twenty feet across, and narrowing as it goes up, with supports zigzagging between each side. The tower stands on its own, no guy wires or other supports. Someone was living up there, or *is* living up there.

I can just hear a distant white noise, a familiar snarling susurration. The Winslow zombies are coming. I don't know what the fresh-brains radar strength is of a horde that big, but even if June pedaled them out of range, they probably kept wandering east until they picked us up again.

I know this is a terrible choice. I know that we will be trapped. I also know that there is no other choice. We can't run. We can't fight. We have to hide.

"It's not far," June says. "Lean on me, Woody, I've got you."

"Are you sure?" I ask.

"What else are we going to do?" June asks as she takes my weight and I shamble forward.

"No. Me," I say. "Infected." The effort and dizziness is making it hard to talk so I use as few words as possible.

"You ever seen anything like this before?" she asks.

"No," I say.

"Okay then," she says. "We don't know what's going to happen, so let's see if we can get you better. We all need to heal up. Let's take some time and come up with a plan."

"A plan," I echo as I stumble forward.

"Talk about the walking dead," Dallas says with a snort when she gets close, moving only slightly faster than me. She's leaning on the bike and hopping along, pushing it over the sandy desert and around the assorted weeds. She's only got one boot on and I can see that her other ankle is badly swollen, the handcuff making a large dent in the swelling. She's making a joke, but it sounds more than a little bit forced and she's got to be in a lot of pain.

"Good to see you too, Dallas," I say between steps.

We make it to the gate into the fenced-off area which is about seventy-by-seventy feet. It has a double gate, wide enough to allow a vehicle in, and while there is a chain wrapped around it and a padlock, the padlock is not locked.

By the time we make it in, and June has left me leaning against the cool side of the small utility building below the tower, I can see the zombies coming.

They are arrayed in a ragged group ranging across the desert and back down to I-40 as far as I can see. Thousands of hungry zombies and only the three of us.

I'm already so sick, but I feel a sinking feeling in my stomach. This is too much. We can't escape from this many. And this was Talia's fallback plan.

She knew I was sick when she dragged me out here and left June and Dallas that crappy clue. Her most hoped for outcome was that June would end up mistaking me for a Z and killing me. Her fallback was that we would be trapped here.

There's something there. Something about that, but my brain is too fogged to figure it out. There are so many and all I want to do is sleep.

The lead zombies walk right into the fence, the dull ringing sound of the fence low against their snarls and snapping jaws, their fetid smell making my guts heave again, only pulling up some of the water I just drank.

"We have to go up," June says gently, taking my arm.

"I... I don't think I can," I say.

"We have no choice," she says. She is tying a rope around my waist, looping it around my legs, forming a makeshift climbing harness. On the end is a length of rope and a carabiner so I can be clipped into the cell tower ladder. I notice she already has on a similar arrangement.

She helps me put on my backpack and I look at the tower. One side has a ladder running up it behind which is the thick, black, snaking cables that run up to the antenna. I hear metal ringing and see that Dallas has started her hopping ascent up the ladder, her bike leaning against the bottom of the tower.

"Shit," I mumble.

"You can do it," June says.

"But should I?" I ask. I hold out my hand. The swelling has come down just a bit but the scratches on my hands and arms aren't right. They are not scabbing up. They are weeping this pink, watery fluid. I've got this moldy taste in my mouth that just won't leave. I nod up and am rewarded with a wave of dizziness. "What if... up there... I...." I say as I cling to her so that I don't fall.

"Then we'll deal with it," she says, holding me up. "But not one second before."

The fence is ringing as more Zs strike it as we are slowly surrounded, as June and I cling to each other. She's holding me. Hard. Like if she lets go, she might lose me. Or maybe that's the way I'm holding her.

"I love you," I whisper, afraid I may never get the chance to say it again. "No matter what happens, remember that I love you."

"I love you too," she says, squeezing me tighter. She doesn't tell me that it will all be alright. She doesn't pretend we aren't in the most desperate of circumstances. That's not my June, and I love her all the more for it.

The ringing of the fence continues. My eyes are closed, but I imagine the Zs stacking up, pressing against the fence. It won't be able to hold them for long.

"If it comes to it," she whispers, "I promise you won't be one of them."

I squeeze her as hard as I can, which isn't all that much, but I can't say anything, my throat too tight. Dallas begged me to promise her something like this back in Winslow and June just up and said it. I feel grateful to her and ashamed of how I was with Dallas.

The snarls get louder and I hear the groan of bending metal. We part and June helps me to the ladder. I clip onto the highest rung I can reach and start the long climb.

CHAPTER EIGHT

THIS IS NOT part of the story I can tell very well, but neither June nor Dallas will write it for me. As the rules of storytelling goes, June would be the best person because of her feelings for me. Even the acerbic and sarcastic Dallas would provide an interesting point of view, but all you've got is me.

And, God, I hope someone, somewhere reads these journals. That the world has time for such leisure and reflection.

And, yes, this is definitely reflection for me, spending all this time scribbling down these thoughts. But it's not leisure. This is required writing, something I have to do to stay sane.

So back to that cell tower in the high desert of Arizona, between Winslow and Holbrook, not far from the Jack Rabbit Trading Post. Back to me being so sick, trying to climb the metal ladder up the cell phone tower one laborious step at a time. Clipping on with each rung I make it up. June right behind me trying to steady me. The sound of zombies pressing against the fence, the smell of them filling my nose, my flesh hot and my head spiking in pain with every heartbeat.

I am infected.

All those scratches I picked up when June dragged me out of the zombie horde on that famous corner in Winslow, Arizona infected me.

Well... To be specific, I'm infected more than I was already infected.

Every living human is infected. I think it goes back to the fungal nature of the zombie invasion. We've all inhaled it, it's gotten in our blood, if we die and our brain remains intact, the fungus takes over and we turn.

It takes a little time, but it is guaranteed.

It's the zombie's bite that everyone is worried about because it must contain some kind of poison that supercharges your existing fungal infection and hastens your death and the fungus taking over.

So, it turns out the scratches of a Z must do something very similar but to a lesser degree. Some kind of substance that once it gets into your bloodstream causes problems.

Thus, I am infected, my immune system under attack and my existing fungal infection attempting to take over.

I don't think of this as I climb. I'm not even really thinking at all, not in the normal sense. It's been the longest, most difficult day of my life—and having survived the apocalypse for over a year, that's saying a lot. I'm beat to hell and infected. I'm dehydrated and exhausted. My lungs are still straining from this morning's smoke inhalation, and I probably have a concussion from where Talia knocked me out.

So, it's one rung at a time with June's gentle encouragement, her sweet voice urging me on, telling me every little thing to do.

"Left leg now, Woody," she says.

I try to do what she is asking but then she says, "No, that's your right foot. Lift your left foot up to the next rung... Good. Now reach up with your left hand and pull yourself up. No. That's your right hand, reach with the hand on this side." And she taps me on my left foot because I'm so far gone that I can't tell my left from my right.

I strain, trying to pull myself up, but I just don't have the strength.

"We got this, Woody," she says gently. Or at least it sounds gentle. If I had been more with it, I suspect I would have heard the strain in her voice. "Let me help you," she says as she scoots up the ladder and gets her shoulder under by butt.

Yes. Quite undignified and most definitely not the kind of thing you want your new girlfriend doing.

"On the count of three," she says, "I need you to push yourself up, okay? One... two... three!"

And on it goes like that with the love of my life treating me like a child, like an invalid, like the very sick and injured person that I am.

I can't tell you how long it takes to get up that ladder. My world has become so small, just June's voice and this long struggle until I am panting and sweating while June pushes me from below and Dallas pulls from above and I flop on the rough plywood floor of the cell tower treehouse.

I am vaguely aware of June on the wood next to me panting and saying, "We made it."

I try to nod my head in agreement, but even that is too much of an effort. I am done. I have nothing left. I promptly pass out and am incoherent for a very long time.

CHAPTER NINE

THIS IS all June's fault.

By "this" I mean this cell tower that we are all stuck in. This "game" of Talia's. This trio of June, Dallas, and me. This desperate situation we are in.

It is all her fault.

I think my fevered brain somehow locks in on this and my journey between consciousness and unconsciousness is very June-centric.

I see her face when my eyes flutter open, worry pulling her lips into a frown and furrowing her forehead while she gets me to take a sip of water or makes me take a pill or helps me eat little bits of food.

She doesn't tell me it's going to be alright. She says things like, "Keep fighting, Woody" or "You can do this" or once when it's dark and I see the Milky Way behind her face and I can't quite keep either in focus, "Come back to me, Woody."

And when I'm not conscious with her, my mind skips back to the moment we met. That cold spring morning on the top of a semi surrounded by hungry Zs at the dog food factory in Flagstaff.

In my fevered mind it's happening all over again.

"Hey, dummy!" she calls from the roof of the plant atop the high cement walls, the bulk of Mount Elden rising behind her where our first adventure occurred.

"Good morning," I yell back, my breath coming out as a cloud on the cold spring morning. I had just woken up on top of a semitrailer surrounded by hungry, snarling, stinking Zs. "I must tell you that I plan to lodge a complaint with management. The room service around here really sucks."

It's an odd thing for me to say to a stranger, but I'm dedicated to humor surviving in this world at least as long as I do.

"You're funny," she replies, but there is no humor in her voice and I want nothing more than to make her laugh. She's far enough away that I can't see her well, but she's not shooting at me or anything, so that's something.

"Thank you very much," I say, taking off my hat and bowing. "I'll be here all week."

"Yeah, you will," she says, eying my predicament. I barely got on top of this semi last night and escaped the Zs. "Want some help?"

"No thank you," I yell back.

"Suit yourself, then. I'll grab some popcorn and watch the show." She pauses briefly, and even from this far away I can see that she is smiling. "And by 'popcorn,' I mean dog food. There's actually some left if you manage to survive."

I had come for the dog food. Any calories in an apocalypse, as the saying goes, and any well-preserved calories doubly so.

And that's it. That's the beginning. A chance meeting of two lone survivors hoping to find some edible dog food. From then on it's been Woody and June versus the Apocalypse.

And Dallas too, who we picked up on day eleven.

June could have not said anything, just watched and seen if I managed to survive. She could have shot me and been done with it. A little bit later, after I safely got down from the semi, she could have let the Zs that surrounded me eat me alive instead of throwing me a rope and blowing one of their heads off so that I could climb up the building and sample the delicious dog food and gaze at her beautiful face for the first time.

And, yeah, dog food is pretty delicious stuff when you are starving.

My brain rewound it all. Without June, I would have gotten off the semi just fine and probably been chased away from the dog food plant by the other Zs there and hiked up Mount Elden alone to visit the lookout tower that I had visited with my old man.

I had been alone for months, and the one goal I had in my mind all that time was to get to Flagstaff, climb the mountain, climb the tower, and see. I somehow hoped that I would get some clarity on my lonely life up there. On what the world had become. On what I should do next.

Without June, I would have run into Brown, the psychotic, petty, wannabe warlord that had an encampment up there and was using the tower to watch over the eastern part of Flagstaff.

And they would have killed me. I wasn't one of them and it was only the capture of June that got my brain moving and had me offering them dynamite I didn't have and had no idea how to get to save her.

I didn't carry a gun. I was obviously not one of them. Very high odds they would have killed me.

My awareness skips between past and present while June gives me sips of water. Dabs at the zombie scratches that just won't heal. Forces me to swallow pills or puts bitter things under my cheek. Warms me with her body in the cold of the night. And when I am unconscious, I keep playing those first two days with June over and over in my mind.

She saved me at the dog food plant and I saved her by rescuing her from Brown and company. And it's been that way ever since. We keep saving each other, and not just physically.

This is not some *It's a Wonderful Life* kind of experience I'm having. First, this is the apocalypse, and while there is plenty to be grateful for, it's the apocalypse. Second, I never doubted how good I had it with June. She is a wonderful woman and an immensely capable survivor. I am lucky to be her friend, much less be with her.

This is my mind reminding me, telling me, showing me what I have to live for. Even if it's just a little more time in the cell tower treehouse until we all starve to death. Any time with June is time worth spending.

And she wants me to survive. It's clear from my glimpses of her that she really wants me to get better so we can continue on this crazy journey.

So, when I say that this is all June's fault, I mean it in the best possible way. It's June's fault that I'm still alive and I have something worth living for. It's June's fault that Dallas has a life outside of Phantom Company. And, yes, it's June's fault that her crazy psychotic, petty, wannabe warlord of an ex is after us and has maneuvered us into this terrible situation.

You take the good with the bad from those you love. And, frankly, the good and the bad are often hard to tell apart and almost always subjective. I have no idea how I'll be classifying Talia's bizarre game once we are clear of it.

So I fight the infection with all I've got. For June, I fight. For our future, I fight. For a chance to get out of this ridiculous situation, I fight.

I fight until it's clear that we are winning, that the fungal infection is receding.

"I've been dreaming of you," I say to June when I wake up and feel like I'm getting better. My tongue isn't so fat and my brain seems to be working. I can hear the zombies shifting below us and smell their fetid scent. I can see the stars above us, twinkling and bright on the clear dark night, the Milky Way a swath of glittering diamonds.

June is pressed against me and we are in a sleeping bag, her warmth filling me up.

"You have?" she asks, her voice just above a whisper, but it sounds like she was awake.

"Yeah," I say. My head hurts, bad, my scratches itch, and I feel as weak as a kitten, but I am conscious and feel a thin thread of hope. "When you ate popcorn and watched me slowly, ever so slowly, take out the Zs around that semi in Flagstaff."

"It was cute," she says.

"Cute?" I ask.

She nods and I feel her push away a little, she's probably trying to get a look at me. "Cute. That little hand weight was pink. You tied it to the end of a rope and spun and spun it whacking them in the head from above."

I chuckle. It's a thin thing, barely there, but it qualifies as laughter for the day, whatever day this might be. And I'm clearly alive and with June, making this a very good day. "That's my girl," I say, "thinking something like that is 'cute.'"

She pauses and I feel her press the back of her hand to my forehead, feel her gently touching my arm where the zombies scratched me. And then she holds me tight and I feel her body quivering. "You are getting better," she whispers.

"Well," I say, holding her back as tightly as my weak body lets. "I can carry on a conversation, so that's something."

She nods and I feel her short hair rubbing against my cheek. This is not a romantic moment, not in the normal sense. A conversation is all I have energy for, and barely that.

"But, cute?" I ask.

She chuckles "Yes, Woody. Cute. No gun, just this slow methodical way of freeing yourself with your little pink hand weight. It showed that you really thought about it. That you were willing to take your time. It was..."

She just leaves it dangling. "It was what?" I ask.

"It was cute," she says with a little giggle. "But it was telling. It was... well, I don't know if I would have thrown you that rope if it hadn't been so cute. If *you* hadn't been so cute."

My breath catches. As an athletic American male in his twenties, "cute" was never a word I liked and certainly not a word I wanted a woman to say or think about me.

Well, that changes right here and now. I love the word "cute." I'll be cute all day long if it's what brought my June to me. If it is what motivated her to give me a chance and saved my life.

As we hold each other, I think about the past month—because I think it has been about a month now—and how dramatically my life has changed. I do some math in my head, quite a feat at this point, and say, "It's been around a month since we met and that means it must be June now. I've decided, it's officially my favorite month of the year."

"See," June says with a small chuckle. "Now that's cute. You're cute."

"Will you guys shut up, and get a freak'n room," a sleepy Dallas says from close by. "Some of us need our beauty sleep."

We all laugh and this time it's real laughter. Quiet, restrained, but real.

We survived the chase across the 40s. We survived the Apache Death Cave. We survived Winslow. And now it looks like I'm going to survive the infection. Sure, we have a hell of a challenge ahead of us, but we are a family now.

"I love you too, Dallas," I say, quite seriously after the laughter has ended.

"Jesus H., Woody," she says. "Stop being so goddamn nice." She pauses and then adds. "I'm really glad you're feeling better."

June and I whisper a little more, I don't really remember about what. I just remember her warmth and her presence as the zombies stir below and the stars glitter above. I remember drifting gently to sleep holding her, filled with hope.

EPISODE 12
WOODY AND JUNE VERSUS THE SEIGE

More adventure, an unthinkable problem, and more Woody and June awaits you in.... *Woody and June versus the Seige*. Available 11/2022

To stay abreast of all things Woody and June, head over to WoodyAndJune.com and sign up for my e-mail newsletter and don't miss out on a thing! Plus, you'll get a free ebook that includes "Park's Law of the Apocalypse," a newsletter-exclusive story in the world of Woody and June.

WOODY AND JUNE VERSUS THE SIEGE

Outnumbered, Four Thousand to Three

Woody Beckman and June Medina defied the odds and found each other in post-zombie-apocalypse Arizona. No longer go-it-alone survivors, they now face the future together with something to lose. Each other.

Stranded in a treehouse built high in a cell tower and surrounded by thousands of zombies, Wood, June, and Dallas face their greatest challenge yet. How do the three of them escape four-thousand starving undead that want nothing more than to make a meal of them?

Can Woody and June beat the odds and let their love flourish in a world of zombies and psychotic, petty, wannabe warlords?

A story of adventure and love and taking things (even the apocalypse) in stride.

BEFORE YOU GO

Before you go, my book, *Bits, Bites, and Rarities: The Worlds of Robert J. McCarter* is a fantastic introduction to my series and worlds. It's only available to my newsletter subscribers, and the price is the best part. It's free!

This action-packed book contains 15 stories, is 750+ pages long, and has 4 exclusive stories that are not available anywhere else, including "Park's Law of the Apocalypse," a story in the world of Woody and June you can't read anywhere else.

Get it today at *RobertJMcCarter.com/newsletter*

ABOUT THE AUTHOR

Robert J. McCarter is the author of more than ten novels and over a hundred short stories. He is a regular contributor to *Pulphouse Fiction Magazine* and his short fiction has also appeared in *The Saturday Evening Post, Andromeda Spaceways Inflight Magazine, Everyday Fiction,* and numerous anthologies.

Robert writes in a variety of genres from contemporary fantasy to science fiction and just about everything in between. His diverse background–including a career in software engineering, growing up on a ranch riding horses, and acting–colors the stories he tells.

He lives in the mountains of Arizona with his amazing wife and his ridiculously adorable dogs.

Find out more at:
RobertJMcCarter.com

BOOKS BY ROBERT J. MCCARTER

WOODY AND JUNE VERSUS THE APOCALYPSE

For a great deal, pick up *Woody and June Versus the Apocalypse* a volume at at time!

Woody and June Versus the Apocalypse: Volume 1 (Episodes 1 - 7)

- Woody and June versus the Wannabe Warlord
- Woody and June versus the Fungus-Head Zombies
- Woody and June versus the Grand Canyon
- Woody and June versus the Ex
- Woody and June versus the Third Wheel
- Woody and June versus Phantom Company
- Woody and June versus the Daring Rescue

Woody and June Versus the Apocalypse: Volume 2 (Episodes 8 - 12) *Coming 2/2023*

- Woody and June versus the Chase (coming 9/2022)
- Woody and June versus Two Guns (coming 10/2022)
- Woody and June versus Winslow (coming 11/2022)
- Woody and June versus the Infection (coming 12/2022)
- Woody and June versus the Siege (coming 1/2023)

Find out more at WoodyAndJune.com

For a great deal, pick up *Neutrinoman & Lightningirl: A Love Story* a season at at time!

Season 1 (Omnibus edition of Episodes 1 - 3)

- Meteor Attack!
- Toxic Asset
- Protocol X

Season 2 (Omnibus edition of Episodes 4-6)

- Off Book
- Hard Times
- Elemental Factors

Find out the latest at Neutrinoman.com

For a complete list of books, go to RobertJMcCarter.com/books

www.ingramcontent.com/pod-product-compliance
Lightning Source LLC
Chambersburg PA
CBHW070650130626
46555CB00006B/2804